JONATHAN'S AMAZING ADVENTURE

Jonathan J. Witherspoon was
angry. He was angry at his
mother. He was angry at his
father. He was angry at his
sister, and he didn't like his dog.

But worst of all, he thought not
one of them liked him.

6

Jonathan wiped away a tear.
After all, he was no baby.

Marnie was the baby. She cried
all the time. If Jonathan said,
"Don't touch that, Marnie. It's
mine," Marnie cried and cried.

8

That very day, she took
Jonathan's new glider plane.

When he tried to take it back,
her face got very red.

Her face always got red when
she was getting ready to cry.

Jonathan tried to explain. He
tried being nice.

"This breaks very easily," he told
her. "See how light it is?"
He patted her arm.
"Don't cry, Marnie. Please."

13

But Marnie would not let go. She
held on to the plane with ten
tiny, strong fingers.

"Mine!" she yelled. "Mine!"
Jonathan pulled one way.
Marnie pulled the other.

Then one of the wings broke off
in her hand. *Snap!*

16

"Now see what you did!" shouted
Jonathan.
He pushed Marnie, and she fell
over.

"Mommy!" she screamed.

Freckles the dog came running
in. Behind him was Jonathan's
mother.

18

Freckles barked at Jonathan.

He licked Marnie's face.

Then Jonathan's mother bent
down and put her arms around
Marnie. She hugged her and
kissed her. She wiped Marnie's
tears away.

"It was an accident," she told
Jonathan. "Marnie is only a
baby. She didn't mean it. She
just doesn't know any better."

Jonathan's mother hugged him.
"We'll fix the wing," she
promised.

But Jonathan turned away.
He was angry. He went outside
and let the door slam.

Jonathan sat on the back steps.
He thought. He thought a lot.
He thought about what it would
be like to run away.

24

He would find a cave and live in
the woods. What fun it would
be! He would catch fish every
day.

He would hunt for wild berries,
climb trees, and explore.

He'd catch the rain in a wooden
cup and drink it when he got
thirsty.

He would make a pillow of moss
and cover himself with leaves.
He would have a wonderful
time.
And he would never be lonesome.
He would make friends with all
the animals—foxes and wolves,
and even a bear! They would
share their food and eat it under
the stars and the moon.

His parents would worry. They
would call and call, "Jonathan,
come home!"
But Jonathan wouldn't come.

Freckles would try to find him.
He would dash around the yard.
He would run up and down the
block. He would lay his head
between his paws and whine.
But Jonathan would be gone.

The seven o'clock news would
tell the story:
"Jonathan J. Witherspoon, a
brave and handsome seven-year-
old boy, has disappeared!"

The radio would announce it—
and the newspapers, too. Every
headline in the land would tell of
the strange disappearance.

People would come from every-
where to join the search.

Special dogs would sniff
Jonathan's blue blanket.

As soon as they got his smell,
they would yip and yowl and run
back and forth.

Then one dog, the biggest of them all, would discover Jonathan's cave. The other dogs would come. They would bark and bark. They would beg Jonathan to go home.

But Jonathan would send them away, saying, "I'll think about it."

Then he would talk it over with
his friends.
Some would tell him to stay. But
his best friend, the bear, would
say, "Go home. Everyone needs
a family, and yours must love
you a lot. Why else would they
try so hard to find you?"

41

Jonathan would give him his
baseball cap.

Then he would say goodbye.

Suddenly, Jonathan found
himself on the back steps.
Something smelled good.
The door opened. Father was
standing there. Mother was
standing there, too.

Inside he could see Marnie.
She was sitting at her special
little table. She smiled and
waved at Jonathan.

Mother held out her hand.
"Come," she said.
"There's pudding for dessert."

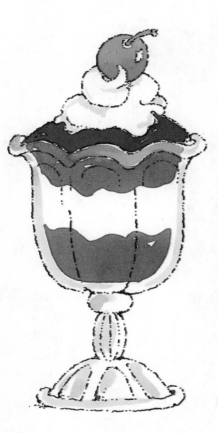

Jonathan took his mother's hand
and went inside for supper—
running away would have to
wait until later!